Santa Farts

Merry Fartmas!

J.B. O'Neil

ISBN: 978-1494242169

Santa Farts

Merry Fartmas!

Table of Contents

FREE BONUS – Santa Farts Audiobook

Hey gang...If you'd like to listen to the hilarious audiobook version of Santa Farts while you follow along with this ebook, you can download it for free for a limited time by going here:

www.funnyfarts.net/santa/

Twas the Night Before Christmas

It was the coldest night of the year, but I was snug and toasty in my stinky bed. When it's cold outside, I like to fart myself a nice warm gas blanket.

I wasn't sleepy though, because I was too excited to sleep. It was Christmas Eve. Santa Claus was coming!

I lay there, listening to the gentle sound of the falling snow. I thought about the presents I might get the next day, and the tasty fart-making foods I'd get to eat.

Hours went by, and I finally felt like I could fall asleep. I rolled over, and I started to have a dream.

I'd gotten a science kit for Christmas, and I invented the world's grossest stink bombs. They were made out of skunk juice, burnt cookies, baby poop, and rotten eggs. They smelled so terrible that when I set one off, everyone in the world said that they would make me King of Earth if I promised not to detonate any more of them. I was a merciful king, and agreed. Then there were no more wars, and everyone was allowed to burp without saying "excuse me."

Suddenly, something startled me awake.

Whatwuzzat!?

It was a fart.

Now, normally I would never be scared by a fart. They're one of my favorite things, after all.

But this fart was different. It was a low, rippling fart, as if it was coming through two wiggly fat butt cheeks. And, it had a distinct rhythm, like laughter. Except, instead of "ho ho ho," it went "thbt thbt thbt."

All these things pointed to the fact that this fart was not mine. Another good piece of evidence was that the noise came from outside my window. I know some really strange and clever farts, but I never throw my farts by accident. I have to do it on purpose. Like when I need to fart at the table and I can blame on my little sister Brittney for it.

Maybe it was a Christmas burglar. What a terrible person, to go sneaking into people's houses on Christmas eve! I was freaking out a little, but I decided I needed to be brave and open the window to get a look outside. I threw back the covers and let out a huge green cloud of warm farts. I would have to remake my fart blanket later.

The Big Man

I hopped on the ice-cold floor over to the window. It was frozen shut, so I had to let out a special, ice-shattering burp to loosen it up. Then I threw up the sash to see what was the matter.

I squinted through the heavy falling snow at the lawn. I didn't think I'd have much luck spotting a burglar if they were wearing black and being sneaky.

I had no problem spotting someone wearing a big red coat and not trying to hide himself.

I blinked, rubbed my eyes, and slapped myself to see if I was dreaming. My cheek hurt. This wasn't a dream.

That was Santa Claus out on the lawn.

Good old Father Christmas himself. Kris Kringel, Sinter Klaus, Jolly Old Saint Nick. Whatever you want to call him, he was *on my front lawn.*

And he was feeding his reindeer a giant can of beans. And laughing while he did it, that classic "Ho Ho Ho!"

Then he farted, "thbt thbt thbt."

I smiled and laughed too. Santa Claus was farting on my lawn and feeding his reindeer baked beans. It was the weirdest, coolest thing I'd ever seen.

To the Top of the Wall!

"Ho Ho Ho! Eat up, you stinky reindeer, eat up! We have lots left to do tonight, and not much time!" Santa said.

When the reindeer had licked the last of the bean juice out of the enormous can, Santa tossed it into his sleigh and hauled himself into his seat. Then he picked up the reins in both hands.

"To the top of the tower, to the top of the wall! Now fart away, fart away, fart away all!" Santa cried, and then the reindeer took off running over the lawn. Suddenly, they all let out a giant reindeer fart, and Santa's sleigh flew up into the air!

I watched it go up, up, up into the sky, then turn around and fly back toward my house.

I heard a loud "thump" on the roof, followed by the clatter of what had to be hooves.

Santa was on top of my house!

I quickly put on my slippers and threw a robe over my pajamas. Then I hurried downstairs to our fire place. I was about to be one of the few lucky kids to ever see Santa Claus, and I intended to not only see him, but meet him!

Milo Meets Santa

I got downstairs just in time to see Santa Claus drop down the chimney and land in our fireplace. He stepped out of the fireplace, dusted off his big red coat, and quietly laughed a "Ho Ho Ho!"

I had meant to run straight up to him and nail him with questions, like "can I wear your hat?" and "how the heck do you get into houses without chimneys?"

But instead, I was totally star struck. I couldn't move or talk. I just stared at Santa with my eyes wide and my mouth hanging open, like a baby looking at jingling keys.

Then he looked right at me. He smiled, and said, "well, if it isn't Milo Snotrocket, the stinkiest boy in the world!"

Santa knew my name!

Instantly my paralysis broke. I dashed into the kitchen, snatched a gallon of milk and a box of cookies, and hurled myself back into the living room. Santa was still there. I thrust out the milk and cookies and tried to say, "here's a snack for you, Santa," but all that came out was "harblegarblegarblegarble!"

I don't take excitement very well.

The Naughty and the Nice

Luckily, Santa didn't think I was some insane kid who needed more medicine than he was getting. He laughed, took my offered snack, and helped himself to the whole box of cookies and the entire gallon of milk. I think at some point I squealed with glee.

Then when Santa was done, he handed me back the empty containers and thanked me. Finally, I could talk again, and I knew what I had to ask

Santa first. But, it was going to be a little uncomfortable.

"Santa, I know you have a list of who is naughty and who is nice. I also know that I tease a lot of people with my farting, and a lot of people don't like it. Am I on your naughty list?"

Santa laughed. "My dear Milo, of course you're not! I love farts! In fact, they're really important for me to do my job. Haven't you ever wondered why I love milk and cookies so much?"

I nodded.

"It's because I'm lactose intolerant. The milk makes me really, really gassy, so I can fart all night! Ho ho ho!"

Clearly, Santa and I were going to get along just fine.

Santa Claus' Sidekick

Santa put my family's Christmas presents under the tree. Then, he filled up all of our stockings. As he worked, he hummed to himself, and every now and then he'd twerk his butt and let out a jolly little fart.

But then, just when he was about to leave, Santa paused. As if he'd just had an idea, and was turning it over in his head to see if it was any good.

"Milo, my boy," Santa said, "I've been wondering for a long time if it might be time for me to be a little more in the open about what I do. How would you like to come with me on my runs tonight, and help me deliver these presents?"

This was it. This was every kid's ultimate dream: being Santa's assistant, his partner, his sidekick! It would be the greatest adventure of my whole life.

"You bet I do!" I said. "Is there anything I need to bring?"

"Get your coat and your boots, and if you have a few cans of beans that your parents won't mind giving to an old man, that would be excellent: the Reindeer get mighty hungry! Ho ho ho!"

Santa Farts #1: The Chimney Sweeper

As Santa had told me, I grabbed my coat, and put on some boots. Then I went to the kitchen, going fast but not as break-neck fast as I'd gone last time. After all, I was sure that Santa wasn't going to just disappear all of a sudden, now that he'd invited me along with him!

I rummaged around until I'd found where Mom keeps the beans. There were all sorts of different kinds, from "classic" to "spicy onion." I took mostly spicy onion. They're my favorite.

Once I had the beans I rejoined Santa in the living room.

"OK Santa, I'm all set. Let's go spread some Christmas!" I said.

"Oh wonderful! Ah, spicy onion, I see. That's my favorite!"

I'm not afraid to admit, I squealed.

When I was done, I realized I had a question. "Hey Santa, how are we getting back up the chimney? Do you use some kind of magic?"

Santa held his belly and laughed merrily. "Ho ho no! Magic? Silly boy, you should already know this trick!"

Then he crouched down and got into the fireplace. He winked at me.

"Elevator going up!" he said, then he let out a giant fart. It shot him straight up the chimney. "Ho ho ho ho!"

I laughed too, and hurried to join Santa on the roof, via the fart express elevator.

Santa Farts #2: The Roof Hopper

Once we'd both gotten up on the roof, Santa took one of the cans of beans into his hand. Then he produced an old can opener from somewhere in his jacket, and quickly opened the beans.

"I just fed them down on your lawn, but since we had that long talk I should top them up!" Santa said. "Looks like they got up to a little 'business' while we were gone too: I hope you parents won't mind reindeer droppings on the shingling! Ho ho ho!"

"Wow, you should have these reindeer wear diapers, Santa," I said, carefully stepping around a brown pile as high as my knee.

"If I did that, then I'd never get this old sleigh off the ground: I'd lose a lot of horsepower! Or should I say, reindeerpower!" Santa said.

After Santa finished giving the reindeer their oniony snack, we hopped into the sleigh.

"Fasten your seatbelt and plug your nose, Milo!" Santa said. "Merry Christmas!"

He snapped the reins, and the reindeer all let out a giant synchronized fart. Santa and I soared through the air, laughing and coughing, to the next house.

Santa Farts #3: The Squeezer

The next house was almost ten miles away, but we got there in seconds. According to Santa, reindeer farts are the strongest fuel in the universe.

We landed on the roof with a thud and a clatter as the reindeer skidded on their hooves. I lurched forward and then was slammed back into my seat.

"I think I'm getting sleigh-sick, Santa," I said, holding my stomach.

"Ho ho ho! If you need to send up your dinner, do it in front of the reindeer: they could always use a snack!" Santa said.

That put me over the edge. The reindeer really did eat it.

When I finished, Santa and I came up to the house's chimney. It was very narrow, more of a smoke stack than a chimney. I figured I could fit, but it would be tight. Santa would have better luck fitting through the hole of a donut.

"I should squeeze down this one Santa," I said. "You can send down the presents one at a time, and I'll put them around the tree."

"What a good boy you are! But there's no need for that: just watch!" Santa said. With a jolly "ho ho ho" he leaped up into the air and dove, head-first, into the chimney, where he promptly got stuck with his feet wiggling in the air.

I was about to grab his legs and pull him out, but then I heard a low hissing noise. Then I smelled something so bad it nearly knocked me over. Through my tears I saw Santa's giant belly deflate like a balloon. Then he slipped down the chimney easily.

Santa Farts #4: Ventriloquism Fart

I jumped down the chimney feet-first, and although I had to wriggle a little, I got down the bottom. Santa was already putting presents under the tree, laughing quietly to himself.

I looked behind me at the hearth, but I saw no stockings there. I pointed this out to Santa.

"The children must have their stockings on their doorknobs to their rooms," Santa whispered knowingly. "We will need to be especially quiet: follow me, Milo, and walk as I do."

Santa then set off down the hall, talking large and exaggerated tip-toe steps. I tried to copy him, but it was actually really hard to walk that way. Soon I was sweating. I'm surprised that Santa is so fat, even though he does eat nearly a ton of cookies on Christmas Eve.

Just as Santa had said, the stockings were on the doorknobs. We filled them up, then tiptoed back the way we'd come. Problem was, my feet got tired, and I accidentally stomped on a loose floor board.

Right away I heard a little kid's voice say "Mom?" and heard a door open behind us. I froze. We were caught!

Just then Santa looked back at me, put a finger to his lips to silence me, and then screwed up his face. He let out a shimmering purple fart, that drifted down the hall to the opening bedroom door.

I heard a woman's voice, and smelled something awful. "Go back to sleep Brad, or Santa won't come tonight."

"OK mom," the kid said, and then the door shut again.

Santa tiptoed up to me and whispered in my ear, "a magical ventriloquism fart. Works every time, ho ho ho!"

Santa Farts #5: The Naughty Child

Later that night, we came to a house that Santa did not seem excited to visit. On the roof he pulled out his giant rolled list of the naughty and the nice, and he checked it carefully.

"This little girl has been *very* naughty for three years in a row now. It breaks my heart to have to skip a child because of their bad behavior, and it's even worse when I have to leave them coal. But this child is so bad, not even coal has caused her to change her ways! I don't know what to do."

I rubbed my chin and thought about the problem. The beauty of Santa's system was that it was shocking and disappointing. When a bad kid thought that they'd get presents and got a lump of coal in a box, it broke their hearts. But no amount of begging or pleading would change what happened: the kid would have to change their ways for a whole year before they'd get another chance.

So what do you with a kid who isn't surprised? You give them something that they can't expect.

"Santa, let me see the box and coal," I said.

Curious, Santa gave me the box. I opened it, and farted my stinkiest, wettest fart. Then I shut the box, trapping the smell inside.

"There: now when she first opens this, the first thing she'll think of won't be coal, but something *else*," I said with a smile.

Santa goggled at me, then threw back his head and let out a "ho ho ho!"

Santa Farts #6: KO Farts

Santa and I working together let us get through houses really quickly. In fact, we started to fall into a steady rhythm: fart onto a house, fart down the chimney, pass out presents, fart up the chimney, repeat. It started to get easy, and we got careless. So careless we nearly got caught.

Santa and I dropped down the chimney and, without even looking, walked right into the living room to put present under the tree.

"Honey? Did you just hear something?"

"Oh snowflakes! Quick Milo, hide!" Santa whispered, and we dashed for cover. Santa hid behind the Christmas tree, and I hid under it.

A couple of parents came into the living room and started sitting and talking on the couch, looking at the tree. They couldn't see us through the needles, but they were in the way. We needed to get them out of there!

Carefully, I looked up through the branches to catch Santa's eye. Then we nodded.

We let out a series of low, soft farts.

"Dear, did you just *sniff*, did you just fart?" the mother said.

"What? Not me, it was you!" the father said.

"Whoever denied it supplied it!"

"Whoever smelt it, dealt it!"

The couple argued, but they gradually grew quieter and quieter, until finally, they fell right asleep.

Tranquilizer farts: perfect for any emergency.

Santa Farts #7: Long Burn

After that close call, the rest of the night went smoothly. Soon we were all out of presents.

"Ho ho ho! It's time to return to the North Pole! Mrs. Claus will be surprised to see me home so soon, I bet. I hope she'll have supper ready!"

I couldn't help feeling sad that the night was over. "I guess it's time for me to get home, huh?"

Santa looked at me, surprised. "My dear Milo, of course not! You must be hungry too. I can't let you leave without tasting Mrs. Claus' cooking, or visiting my workshop! You're coming with me, if you want to."

Of course I wanted to. This was possibly a bigger deal than helping deliver the presents!

"Get out the biggest cans of beans Milo, we're going to have to make a long burn to make it all the way north," Santa said. We fed all the reindeer, and ditched all the extra weight in the sled like empty cans.

"Here goes! Ho ho HO!" Santa cried, and he snapped the reins. The reindeer galloped to the edge of the roof, let out the biggest fart yet, and we were suddenly airborne, soaring high over the earth on our way to the north pole.

Santa Farts #8: Factory Farts

We flew for what felt like hours, but I'm not sure if time passed at all. My watch stopped, and it never seemed to get darker or lighter in the sky. The stars hung where they were, and the moon was always visible. To be direct: it was pretty weird.

At last we started to drop altitude, and I could see lights on the ground, outlining what looked like a landing strip. I could barely see people waving lightsticks to guide us in. As we touched down, I saw that they weren't people. They were short, and wore pointy green hats. They were Santa's elves!

We got out and were escorted by six little green elves straight to Santa's workshop. I expected a little house, but this was a full-sized factory. And it smelled *horrible*.

"Ugh, Santa, this isn't right! You're polluting a whole lot!"

"Ho ho ho! Not so, Milo!" Santa said cheerfully. "What you're smelling is 100% organic fart-power! The fumes are fart emissions. Smelly, but natural: I've made my toys this way for a hundred years!"

Fart power. I never would have guessed that farts could make children around the world so happy. I wondered how Santa got the smell out of the toys...

Santa Farts #9: Elf Farts

We went inside the factory. A tiny elf wearing huge glasses brought a clipboard to Santa, and Santa started to inspect the factory and check things off. I tagged along, but Santa didn't talk very much. I started to get a little bored, and went to watch the elves work.

Mostly they did the stuff you'd expect: they put toys together on conveyer belts, pulled switches, and pushed buttons. I was seriously starting to think that Santa's workshop was the biggest letdown since the temporary tattoo, until something went wrong.

An elf got their sleeve caught on the belt, and got pulled onto the track. He was heading right for a gauntlet of mechanized sewing needles!

But the elf didn't scream or panic. Instead, he let out a giant, vibrant red fart. It shot up into the air like a flare, and then a bunch more red farts shot up. In two seconds, the sounds of the machines started to slow, then stop: the factory was shut down.

Then other elves helped the trapped elf out of the belt. When they were done, they shot out green farts, and the factory started up again. It all took less than 10 minutes.

I made a mental note to myself right there: if I ever wanted to be rich when I grew up, I'd run a factory with fart-based safety systems!

Mrs. Claus' Midnight Meal

Santa finished his inspection and ordered his elves to collect a few more toys: he'd missed a few houses and would have to make a quick final run. "When I do that, I'll take you home Milo," Santa said to me, "but first, it's time for some supper! I can smell Mrs. Claus' cooking from here!"

We trudged through the deep snow and the dark to a little log cabin. Inside it was warm and toasty. I saw a big old woman with glasses and her white hair tied up in a bun. She looked like everyone's favorite grandma: it was Mrs. Claus!

"Hoo hoo hoo! Hello my little cookie, Santa brought you all the way here, did he?" Mrs. Claus said to me. "You must be dreadfully cold. Hurry to the kitchen now, and I'll make you a big warm plate of supper."

"Gee, thanks Mrs. Claus!" I said. "What's to eat?"

"Santa's favorite of course: pickled eggs, pickled beets, and hot beans and franks! Hoo hoo hoo!"

"Ho ho ho!"

"Hoo hoo hoo!"

Then Mrs. Claus let out a big toot. I guess she liked farting as much as Santa!

Home Stinky Home

I'd loved staying at Santa's cabin. Mrs. Claus stuffed me with farty foods, and I soon felt warm and sleepy. But Santa just patted his belly, kissed Mrs. Claus, then stood up.

"Ho ho ho! I know you're very tired Milo, but we must be getting on. It will be dawn soon, and I must finish my rounds! And you, I'm afraid, must go home."

I nodded sleepily and got up. Mrs. Claus dressed me up snug in my coat, and gave me a hat like

Santa's to keep me warm. I stumbled out into the dark, with Santa right behind me.

We got into the sleigh and Santa flicked the reins. We flew up, up, and away, and as we flew I thought about all the amazing things I'd seen that Christmas eve. The moon shone brightly, the stars shimmered, and the sleigh rocked gently back and forth. I soon fell asleep.

Suddenly, I was startled awake. I was in my own bed, with my pajamas on. Had it all been a dream?

I shivered: the window was open, and snow was blowing in. I got up to shut it, and spotted a shadow in the sky. It looked like a sleigh, pulled by flying reindeer.

And I heard a voice, but it might have been the wind:

"Merry Fartmas to All, and to All, A Good Fart! HO HO HO!"

Merry Fartmas!

I must have fallen asleep again, because I opened my eyes in my bed. It was morning: Christmas morning!

I leapt out of bed and looked around my room. The whole night had felt like a dream, but yet not quite. I wanted to find proof that I'd really been with Santa. If I could find the hat Mrs. Claus gave me...

But it was nowhere to be found. My coat was hung up on the hook in my room like normal, and there was no melting snow anywhere.

Maybe it *had* been a dream. I felt sad, but not much. After all, it was still Christmas!

I met my family at the Christmas tree, and we all opened our presents. Brittney got a lego set to build a house for her dolls, and I got my science kit! I was going to make so many stink bombs!

But when we were all done, I noticed that there was one more present, hiding deep under the tree. It wasn't very big, and there was a single word written on the green wrapping paper: "Milo."

My family watched curiously as I opened the slim box. When I lifted the lid, I was hit by a smell so powerful tears popped into my eyes.

When I could see more clearly, I saw that it was the hat that I had gotten from Mrs. Claus. My very own, super stinky Santa hat.

Maybe it had been a dream, but don't they say that dreams can come true?

More Books by J.B. O'Neil

Hi Gang! I hope you liked "Santa Farts." Here are some more funny, cool books I've written that I think you'll like too...

http://jjsnip.com/fart-book

And...

http://jjsnip.com/booger-fart-books

Silent but Deadly...As a Ninja Should Be!

http://jjsnip.com/ninja-farts-book

Did you know cavemen farted?

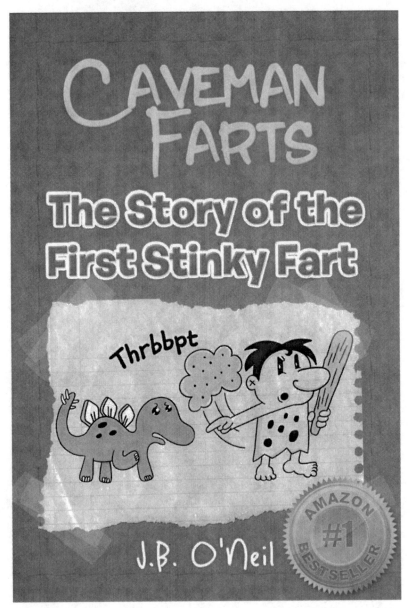

http://jjsnip.com/caveman-farts

Think twice before you blame the dog!

http://jjsnip.com/dog-farts

A long time ago, in a galaxy fart, fart away...

http://jjsnip.com/fart-wars

It's a turd, it's a sewer, no! It's...

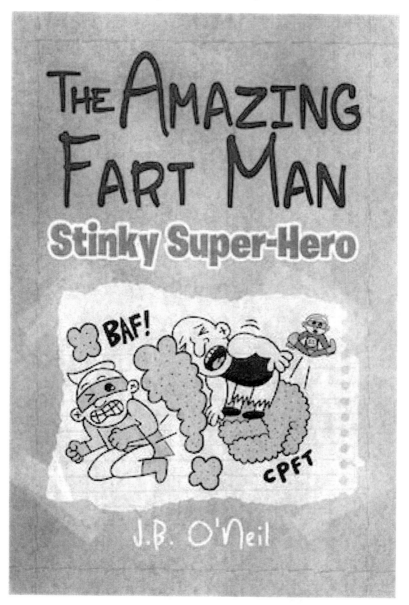

http://jjsnip.com/fartman

We Are the Farts! The Mighty Fighting Farts!

http://jjsnip.com/fart-ball

Farts can be Spooky, too:

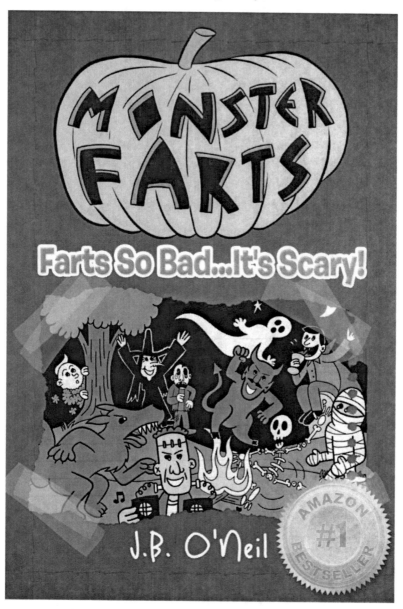

http://jjsnip.com/monster-farts

CPSIA information can be obtained at www.ICGtesting.com
Printed in the USA
LVOW10s1719071215

465787LV00021B/1386/P